Tarzan, King of the Apes

Edgar Rice Burroughs

TARZAN
King
of the Apes

Adapted by
Joan D. Vinge
from *Tarzan of the Apes*

Random House
New York

1

John Clayton, Lord Greystoke, was a very worried man. The small trading ship on which he was a passenger lay at anchor off a nameless cove, miles from any outpost of civilization. Far in the distance the shoreline met the dense, lush green of the mysterious West African jungle. *Terra incognita*, thought Greystoke. Unknown lands. He knew almost nothing about the vast continent whose shores he watched; few Europeans did. And for the first time since he had begun this journey, his lack of knowledge frightened him.

It hadn't worried him when he had been offered a post in Africa by the Colonial Office in London. He was being sent to investigate the mistreatment of black British subjects in a British African colony by the European power that controlled a bordering African state. The mission was a delicate one, because the European power was friendly to England. But Greystoke was young, confident, and proud to be entrusted with such a responsibility. He had never been to Africa, but he was a former army officer, and he was sure that he could handle any difficulty the Dark Continent had to offer. After all, it was 1888, he was an Englishman, and the British Empire ruled the seas.

But he hadn't realized how alone and isolated an Englishman could feel in the far reaches of the Empire—not until he had found himself aboard this trading ship, which was run with an iron fist by a callous brute of a captain and manned by some of the worst ruffians he had ever seen in any port. And he had never imagined that the crew would mutiny and he would find himself in a position like this. . . .

Now, watching the ship's sullen crew stacking up crates of provisions and belongings, Greystoke felt helpless and small for the first time since he was a child.

It wasn't for himself that he was worried, but for the ship's most precious passenger—his new wife, Lady Alice. He should never have allowed her to come with him to Africa. This was no place for a gentle, well-bred Englishwoman! A land of savage beasts and strange diseases, the sweltering, uncivilized end of the world.

He frowned more deeply as he remembered how he had told those things to Alice again and again at home in England. She should remain at Greystoke, he had said, and oversee the ancestral estates like a proper lady of the manor. But she had insisted on going with him. They had not been married long, and she refused to be separated from him now that they had vowed to be together all their lives. And because she was so beautiful and so full of life, because he loved her as much as she loved him, he had finally agreed to let her come to Africa.

"John!"

He turned and saw her coming toward him along the deck. Strands of her fair, upswept hair whipped about her worried face. The sight of her made his heart fill in spite of his concern. "Alice, you should stay below! God knows whether these ruffians will keep their promise—"

"Oh, John." She shook her head stubbornly as she reached his side. "I had to be sure that you were still safe up here."

He put his arm around her and kissed her gently on the cheek. Through their whole difficult journey she had never complained about their rude accommodations or the heat, though he knew she must have felt the discomfort even more than he did because of her heavy skirts and stays. But now their precarious situation made all that had happened before seem as unimportant as a summer rain.

"Soon we'll be ashore," he said as confidently as he could, "and we'll be rid of this misbegotten lot." He feared that worse dangers awaited them in the jungle, where the mutineers were leaving them, but he did not say so. Though it was a grim fate to be left ashore, Greystoke knew that he and Alice were lucky. The crew might have murdered them, along with the captain and the ship's officers, after the bloody battle that had taken place only two days before. They were fortunate; their lives had been spared.

Alice's clear gray eyes met his, as if she sensed the concern he was trying to hide from her. But she only nodded, looking thoughtfully at the shore.

Just then the leader of the mutineers approached them. He was a huge, burly man with a heavy black mustache; the other men called him Black Michael. By an accident of fate, Clayton had saved his life several days before. Black Michael had tried to stop Captain Billings from beating an old sailor, and the captain had almost killed Black Michael with his revolver. But Clayton had struck the gun aside, earning the captain's wrath and Black Michael's grudging gratitude.

And so, when the crew at last rebelled against their cruel officers, Lord Greystoke and his lady had been warned to stay below, and Black Michael himself had seen to it that they were not harmed.

But they were still far from safe. Instead of taking them to the nearest port, Black Michael had told them that he intended to strand them here, at this uninhabited bay.

"We'll be putting you ashore now," he said gruffly, standing before them.

Clayton took a deep breath and tried to

change the mutineer's mind. "We're grateful to you for sparing our lives. Surely you know that. But for God's sake, man, can't you at least put us ashore on some more hospitable coast? Near enough to civilization so that we might at least hope to find our way to safety?"

Black Michael shook his head. "I am the only man aboard who would not rather see ye dead. I know that's the sensible way to make sure of our own necks, but Black Michael's not the man to forget a favor. Ye saved my life once and I'm goin' to spare yours, but that's all I can do. The men won't stand for any more.

"I'll put all your stuff ashore with ye, as well as supplies enough to last ye until ye can find fruit and game. With your guns for protection, ye ought to be able to live here easy enough until help comes. When I get safely away, I'll see to it that the British government learns about where ye be."

Clayton said nothing more, knowing it was useless. He did not believe that Black Michael had the slightest intention of notifying the British government of their whereabouts. He was not even sure that some treachery wasn't being planned for when they were put ashore; but there was nothing he could do except wait and see.

As it turned out, Black Michael himself oversaw their landing and then left with the last boat after all their belongings were safely high and dry. Because they had been expecting a five-year stay at their new post, they had packed dozens of trunks and boxes. Black Michael had decided that nothing belonging to the Claytons should be left on board his ship—though whether he did it out of compassion for them, or merely self-interest, would have been hard to say. If the property of a missing British official had turned up on board the mutineers' suspicious vessel, they would be in serious trouble in any civilized port.

As the last boat moved slowly over the smooth waters of the bay, back toward its parent ship, the Claytons watched its departure in silence. At first neither one of them had the heart to speak the words that filled their minds.

Finally John Clayton pushed his dark hair back from his eyes and said quietly, "Well,

we're stranded here alone, just the two of us."
He put his arms around Alice. "But thank
God we still have each other."

Alice rested her head on his shoulder.
"Someone will search for us, won't they?
When we don't arrive, someone will send out
another ship. . . ." She tried to keep her
voice steady as she looked out at the empty
sea, calm and sparkling under a sky bright
with the morning sun.

"Of course," John said. "They'll search for
us. But . . . you understand, it may take
some time to find us. This coast is so long
and uninhabited."

She lifted her head to look at him. "You
think they'll never find us."

"I didn't say that—"

"You think we'll be here forever!"

"Alice—"

She burst into tears. Anger at her own
weakness only made her cry harder.

"Darling, we'll be all right. I'll take care
of you."

"You don't understand!" She wiped her
eyes, shaking her head. "I'm fine anywhere,
as long as I have you. But, John, I'm going
to have a baby!"

"What?" he said, letting go of her in amazement. "A baby?" He stared at her waist, but she knew that nothing showed yet. She had done her best to keep that secret life hidden from him these past weeks. "How long have you known?"

"Since before we left England," she said, feeling calmer now that the truth was out at last.

"Why didn't you tell me?" he almost shouted, torn between joy and anguish.

"Because you'd never have let me come if you knew." Her eyes filled with tears again. "Would you?"

"Of course not," he snapped. But then his arms were around her again; he held her and their child close to his heart. After a moment he let her go and looked toward the jungle at their backs. Bright-colored birds soared over the beach, and strange creatures called from the rustling, hidden depths of the trees. The exotic scents of a hundred nameless flowers filled the air. The jungle was a place of unknown, terrifying secrets. And yet it was also a place of great beauty.

"Perhaps this is what Eden was like, John," Alice said softly.

John touched the shining hair that lay loose across her shoulder. "This will be our new home. We'll build a fine house here, a safe and sturdy one, for ourselves and our child. But first we'll need a safe shelter for tonight or we'll make breakfast for some wild beast."

John worked through the day to make them a rough shelter high in the branches of a tree. Alice did all that she could to help him, despite his protests about her delicate condition. And despite his protests, he was secretly glad to have her help.

That night they slept fitfully in their aerie high above the ground while below them in the darkness unseen creatures snuffled and growled their hunger and curiosity. And all through the night the cries of the hunter and the shrieks of the hunted, the snappings and rustlings of the restless jungle, never ceased.

They woke to a new morning, feeling as if they had barely slept at all. But their spirits rose with the sun, and they began to explore their surroundings. They searched along the beach and the jungle's edge for anything that would help them adapt to their new life.

They found tide pools among the rocks, filled with small, flitting fish and edible seaweeds. The jungle offered them fruits and berries and the promise of game, and a clear stream flowed out of its depths and down to the cove. They laughed like children as each new discovery gave them more confidence in their ability to survive in the wild.

In the weeks and months that followed, their days took on a rhythm and routine, until the strangeness of their new life began to seem almost natural and their former life as distant as a dream. John began to keep a diary, written in French, as he had done for years. In it he sometimes despaired, for no rescue ship ever appeared on the horizon and his wife grew ever more pregnant. But Alice seemed to blossom spiritually as well as physically in her new life as she learned to weave and fish and cook over an open fire. When he watched her now, he was quite amazed; and he found that the pride and love he felt for her grew stronger with the passing days. Watching Alice lifted his own spirits and gave him fresh hope.

He built them the sturdy home he had promised, plank by plank and stone by stone.

The small cabin stood at the jungle's edge, as solid as a castle, and they slept soundly inside it, no longer bothered by the terrifying sounds of the night.

They befriended some of the smaller creatures of the jungle, especially the birds and the playful, chattering monkeys who wandered down to the beach, unafraid of humans because they had never seen one before. Occasionally some predator, a leopard or a lion, ventured out from the forest's edge; but such creatures rarely appeared in the daytime, and they quickly learned to fear John's skill with a pistol.

From time to time John and Alice had glimpsed another sort of creature watching them from among the trees. Because they were covered with hair and gave hooting animal cries as they disappeared into the forest, John guessed that they were apes, the humanlike beasts that had caused such a scandal back in England when the biologist Charles Darwin had claimed they were first cousins to human beings. John laughed with Alice at the thought that they—or anyone else—could ever mistake apes for humans, even savage ones.

As time passed, John felt so safe from attack that he began to leave the house without a weapon. Then one morning, as he collected wood by the jungle's edge, he came face-to-face with an ape for the first time. The ape stood frozen, its hair standing on end and its teeth bared. It was a far larger animal than John had imagined—much heavier than he was, with massive arms that could easily break his own in two. He had only his hatchet with him, and he knew that it wouldn't be enough to save him. And then what would happen to Alice? Suddenly the safety of the cabin seemed a hundred miles away. He began to back up slowly, hoping that the ape might let him go.

But as he moved, the ape sprang after him. He turned and ran, the ape following him furiously down the beach. He had nearly reached the cabin when he saw Alice step outside. He shouted at her to go back in and bolt the door, and she disappeared inside just as the ape caught up with him, bowling him over. He struggled to his feet, bruised and bleeding, clutching his hatchet helplessly as the ape lunged at him again. Its heavy hands wrenched the hatchet from his own, hurled it away, and reached for his throat. Suddenly there was the loud crack of a rifle shot, and the ape staggered in mid-attack. It turned, snarling in pain and rage. Past its shoulder John glimpsed Alice standing with the rifle in her hands.

The ape saw her, too, and before John knew what was happening, the beast was rushing toward her. "Alice!" John shouted, frantic with fear. She tried to fire again, but before she could, the ape was on top of her. John followed, throwing himself at the ape like a madman, trying to pull it off her.

The ape's body rolled limply to the ground. The bullet had done its work; the ape had been dying even as it had attacked her.

"Alice," John gasped, lifting her head, cradling her in his arms. "Are you all right?"

Her face was twisted with pain, but he could see no injury anywhere on her. Her hands rose to press her stomach—and then he understood.

That night a son was born in the tiny cabin beside the primeval forest while a leopard screamed in the distance and a lion's roar echoed from beyond the ridge.

Lord and Lady Greystoke lived in peace and happiness for several more months, reveling as each new day brought more delightful changes in their infant son. The apes still watched from the trees, but neither John nor Alice ever left the cabin again without a weapon. They had learned the lesson of the wild well, and they were content.

But there were dangers in the tropical jungle that no one could guard against or even see—and at last Alice fell ill with a fever. John had no medicines to treat her. He could only watch helplessly as she slipped away, until she no longer recognized him or their child. Then one night he woke to the roar of rain and the crash of thunder, to the wailing of their child, and found that Alice would never stir from their bed again. She was dead.

He stumbled to the baby's cradle and picked up his son; he stood there in a daze as lightning lit the still form of his beloved wife. The baby nuzzled hungrily at his chest, crying to be fed. "Oh, Alice, Alice," John murmured brokenly. "What shall I do without you?"

2

A mile back from the ocean, deep in the jungle, Kerchak the ape, the leader of his band, sprang wildly from tree to ground and back again. The storm's fury had driven him into a frenzy, and the other apes of the band fled, hooting and screaming in fright, as he attacked. Any ape not quick enough to escape was torn by his vicious teeth or battered by the heavy branch he wielded in his powerful fist. When other males began to imitate his frenzied dance, the females of the tribe clutched their young protectively to their chests or hoisted them onto their backs.

An ape named Kala, trying to guard her infant from the madness on all sides, suddenly found her child wrenched from her arms by the raging Kerchak. She leaped frantically after him into the trees, biting him on the neck and sweeping her child to safety in her arms. She sprang away again, but Kerchak followed her from tree to tree, biting and pummeling her, enraged by her defiance. Finally a branch snapped beneath her weight, and she tumbled toward the ground. She managed to break her fall by catching hold of a limb, but the impact tore her clinging infant loose from her. She watched helplessly as it fell to the rocks far below.

Screaming her grief, she leaped down through the branches to the ground and lifted her lifeless infant in her arms. She was a young ape, and the child she had just seen fall to its death was her first. She cradled the lifeless body while she stroked it and whimpered. Holding it futilely against her breast, she tried to shelter it from the pouring rain.

Kerchak watched her from the trees, his fit of rage forgotten at the sight of the dead infant. He came down slowly to the ground and tried to approach Kala. Kala turned her back on him, and he moved away again.

Gradually the other apes came down from their refuges as they realized that Kerchak's frenzy was over. Young apes began to leap and play. Some of the adults rested on the soft mat of decaying vegetation that covered the ground beneath the trees, and others rooted under branches and rocks for insects and small lizards to eat.

As dawn brightened the sky, the storm moved on, and so did the apes. Kerchak led them through their territory down to the edge of the sea, where they fed cautiously on figs and leaves, keeping a wary eye on the hut and the hairless white apes they had come to fear. Kala ate little and sat apart from the others with her dead infant still clutched against her. She stared out at the sea, until at last her sensitive ears caught a sound that made her stir: a baby's cry.

She climbed down from her perch in the tree and started toward the cabin, the source of the cry. For once its door stood open and unguarded. Kerchak and the others watched her in surprise. She drew closer and closer, but no invisible death leaped out to strike her down. Kerchak climbed out of his tree and followed her, drawn to the cabin by curiosity and vanity. He couldn't let the other apes think that he was afraid to go where a mere female went. Slowly the others followed his lead.

Inside the cabin John Clayton sat at his desk, numbly recording his wife's death in his diary. Behind him the baby had quieted again, sucking its fingers in a futile effort to soothe its hunger. And in the hot noontime silence John heard another sound—the questioning grunt of an ape.

He turned slowly in his seat. An enormous ape stood in the doorway of the cabin, with others behind it, staring back at him. For a moment he sat paralyzed, as if waiting for fate's hand to strike him down. But then the baby began to cry again, and his trance was broken. He leaped up and lunged across the room toward his pistol and rifle, which hung on the far wall.

Kerchak charged, sweeping Clayton up in his powerful arms. He hurled the man over his head and into the wall with such force that beams cracked. Kerchak lifted the man's body again. Then he dropped it when he saw that his victim was already dead.

The baby began to scream in its cradle, and Kerchak started toward it, grunting a threat. But Kala was there before him and snatched the baby away just as he reached for it. As she caught up the human child, her own dead infant dropped into the cradle. Swiftly Kala bolted through the doorway and across the beach, taking refuge in a tree.

High up among its branches she hugged the shrieking infant to her breast, stroking and soothing it with motherly love. Gradually the baby quieted, and hunger closed the gap between them as the son of an English lord and lady began to nurse at the breast of Kala the ape.

In the meantime Kerchak and several other apes rummaged curiously through the belongings of the dead man and woman who lay in the cabin. The rifle hanging on the wall caught Kerchak's attention. Dimly he recognized it as the stick that delivered invisible death to apes and other creatures. Now it was his to investigate. He approached it nervously, then backed away, ready to run if it spoke or spat fire. He hooted and paced and thumped his chest in warning, but it made no response. At last he reached out for it with an immense hairy hand. He snatched his hand away again as he touched the cold metal.

Again and again he touched the gun, until finally he tore it from its hook and held it firmly. When it did not harm him, he began to examine it. He peered down the black depths of the muzzle, fingered the sights, the breech, the stock, as the other apes watched—and finally he touched the trigger.

The gun fired with a deafening roar, and the onlooking apes fell over one another in their desperate rush to get out of the door and away.

Kerchak himself was so frightened that he ran from the cabin, holding the rifle. As he bolted outside, the muzzle caught the edge of the open door, slamming it shut behind him. Kerchak came to a halt a little way from the cabin and realized that he still held the gun. He dropped it like a burning branch and fled with the others.

It was an hour or more before the apes could bring themselves to approach the cabin again to continue their exploration. When they finally reached its doorway, they found the door shut and locked so securely that they couldn't force it open. Finding that there was no other way into the cabin, they started back to the deeper forest.

Kala had not once come down from the trees with her adopted baby, but now Kerchak called to her as the band left the shore. There was no anger in his voice, and so she joined the rest in returning home.

The next day the other apes began to try to examine Kala's strange baby. She drove them away with bared teeth until they convinced her that they meant the infant no harm. Then she let them come close, but she would not let them touch her child, as if she sensed that her baby was frail and delicate and feared that the others might injure him accidentally.

Other infants rode on their mothers' backs, their arms wrapped tightly around their mothers' necks. But Kala's child was too young to ride that way and so, when they traveled, she held the baby protectively against her chest with one hand. He clung to her fur tightly with tiny, naked fists. It made traveling hard and awkward for her, but she remembered her own baby's fall too clearly.

She would not let anything happen to this one.

Kala cared tenderly for her little waif and never lost patience with him, even though he seemed to be hopelessly backward compared to the infants of other mothers. While their young were leaping and running, he could barely walk. Having to guard and protect and carry him constantly left Kala weary and often without her own fair share of food and companionship. Even Tublat, her mate, snarled at the child and threatened him constantly. Other apes urged her to leave the weakling behind so that she could bear other, stronger babies.

She ignored them all, determined to protect and carry little Tarzan—which meant "White Skin" in the language of the apes—forever if she had to. She would never give him up. She tickled him and groomed him, soothed his hurts and fears, and encouraged his struggles to learn the ways of a normal ape.

And her faith in him was rewarded as he slowly began to do all the things other young apes did—to walk and run and even climb a little. Kala showed him how to hunt for grubs and lure termites from their mounds with a twig, what leaves and fruits were safe to eat, and how to follow the tracks of other creatures. Her child learned to remember those things very easily, much to her surprise. But countless moons passed and he still stared up wistfully at his young friends as they swung effortlessly from branch to branch high in the trees. Sitting on a rock below, he was barely able to reach the lowest limb.

As more time passed he eventually began to swing from tree to tree also, though never as well as other young apes his age. But then he began to do things Kala had never taught him, things she had never seen any ape do. He quickly learned the apes' simple language of grunts and hoots and gestures, and learned to placate his larger and stronger playmates and the adults to whom he was still a nuisance and a weakling. But he made other noises as well—strange unapelike babblings that only caused the other apes to draw away from him suspiciously. Kala sensed his disappointment and frustration when his need to make noises only caused the others to mistrust him more. But even she could not understand why he made them, and so she was helpless to comfort or encourage him when he did.

After a while the noises stopped; but then Tarzan began to imitate the voices of other creatures and birds with startling clarity. He quickly learned to use his gift of mimicry to play tricks on his friends and tormentors alike, imitating a leopard's cough or a lion's growl to frighten them away from food and startle them out of their nests as they slept. When they realized what he had done—always too late—they would chase him, waving branches and snapping their teeth. But when they did, he would drop to the ground and run, hooting with laughter, outdistancing them easily. Even though he could never equal their agility as they swung through the trees, he was far quicker and more graceful than they were on the ground.

As more time passed he taught himself other tricks no ape had ever dreamed of before. He learned to hurl rocks and branches with amazingly good aim. He even learned to wrap a piece of tough vine back on itself to form a loop that pulled tight, trapping anything it was dropped over. Once he had mastered the loop, his practical jokes became even more wicked. He especially liked to lay traps for the bully Tublat, Kala's mate, who had always hated him and frequently abused him when Kala was not around. Now that Tarzan was old enough and clever enough to take revenge, he made Tublat's life miserable. Nooses and snares would drop out of trees or lie underfoot when the old ape least expected them, then yank him into the air. Strange noises would terrify him; nuts would rain down out of the trees onto his thick skull. And then he would see that miserable, hairless creature hooting at him from high up in the slender branches that would never hold his own weight. Kala could do nothing with the child; even Kerchak, the leader of the band, got only token displays of submission from him. Tublat wished again and again that he had strangled Tarzan when the child was still an infant.

3

By the time Tarzan was ten years old, he had become an excellent climber and could do many things on the ground that were impossible for his little brothers and sisters. His cleverness amazed them, even though he was still puny physically and no match for their strength. By ten the apes were almost adults, while Tarzan was still a half-grown child.

And yet, compared to other human children, the boy was amazingly strong and fit, since he had spent years swinging from branch to branch through the trees and running, playing, and wrestling with his bigger and stronger friends. By the time he was ten, he could leap twenty feet from the highest limbs of one tree to another, catching the branches with unerring precision. He could drop from limb to limb of a tree, gliding fluidly down to the ground, or climb to the top of the tallest of trees with the ease and swiftness of a squirrel. And every day he grew stronger.

His life among the apes was happy, for he had no memory of any other life and no idea of the greater world that existed beyond his own stretch of jungle.

He was nearly eleven before he even began to think about what a great difference there was between himself and the other apes. His small body, browned by the sun, suddenly made him feel terribly ashamed as he realized that it was entirely hairless, like a snake's or a reptile's, and not a proper ape's.

He even tried to disguise his hairlessness by plastering mud all over himself, but the mud only dried and fell off. Besides, wearing mud was so uncomfortable that he quickly decided he preferred the shame to the discomfort.

On the high plateau where the band of apes spent much of their time was a small lake where they drank during the dry season. One day, crouching on the bank beside one of his cousins, Tarzan studied his reflection in the water. He had never thought about his own face before, always assuming that it looked like any other ape's. But now he saw the truth, and he was appalled. It had been bad enough to be hairless, but to look like this . . . !

That tiny mouth with its puny little teeth—it looked ridiculous compared to the wide jaws and long, sharp teeth of his luckier friends. And that pinched little nose was so narrow that it made him look half starved! He glanced at his cousin's reflection, seeing the beautiful, broad nostrils that covered half his face. Tarzan thought miserably that it must be wonderful to be so handsome.

But looking into his own eyes was the final blow. A black spot, a gray circle, and then blank whiteness. Not even snakes' eyes were so hideous!

He was so preoccupied with his own ugliness that he did not hear the rustle of the tall grass parting behind him. Neither did his cousin, sucking and gurgling water noisily at Tarzan's side.

Sabor the lioness crouched not thirty steps

behind them, lashing her tail. She moved forward cautiously on her huge padded paws, her belly to the ground—a great cat preparing to leap at its prey.

Now she was only ten feet behind them. She flattened, then drew her feet in. Her muscles bunched beneath her glossy hide; her lashing tail stilled. For an instant she hesitated, as if she had turned to stone. And then, with a terrible scream, she sprang.

Her wild scream was not a warning; it was meant to freeze her victims with terror for the moment it would take her to reach them, until she could sink her claws in and hold them helpless.

And for the young ape her strategy worked perfectly. He crouched, paralyzed and trembling, for just an instant—and that was long enough to be his undoing.

But not Tarzan's. All his life the human child had been learning to use his mind to protect his weaker body—and now Sabor's scream inspired him.

Behind him was certain death, but before him lay the great waters of the lake. Like the apes, Tarzan had always hated water. It was cold, wet, elusive stuff, fit only for drinking.

His mother had always taught him to stay away from it, and he had seen little Neeta disappear beneath its treacherous surface only a few weeks before.

But it was the lesser of two evils, and before Sabor had completed half her leap, Tarzan felt the chill waters of the lake close over his head.

He could not swim, and the water was very deep; but he kicked his way to the surface instinctively, gasping for breath. More by accident than by plan, his thrashing arms began to dog-paddle. In a few seconds he discovered that he could keep his head above water and even move forward through it if he kept paddling and kicking. He was amazed and delighted by the new skill that fate had thrown his way, but he had no time to think much about it now. He swam parallel to the bank, seeing the lioness crouched over the motionless form of his friend. Sabor watched him intently, as if she expected him to come back to the shore; but he had no intention of doing that. Instead he began to scream the distress call of the apes, and a warning that would put rescuers on their guard.

He heard an answering call, and soon most

of his band came swinging through the trees toward the lake. Kala was in the lead, having recognized the voice of her best-loved child, and with her was the mother of his dead cousin.

The lioness raised her head as she heard them come and she snarled with rage. Knowing that she was outnumbered, she took the limp body of the ape child in her jaws and bounded away into the jungle.

Tarzan swam to the shore and scrambled onto the bank. His astonished mother hugged and stroked him, grunting her relief and wonder. Beside them the mother of the lost child shrieked with grief as the rest of the band tried to comfort her.

When he had time to recover and to think about his new discovery, Tarzan returned to swim in the lake again. Soon he learned to leap from the trees and plunge deep into the lake's cool waters, delighting in his new-found skill. Kala could only watch him incredulously from the shore. Tarzan could never lure any of his friends in to join him, but even that could not spoil his pleasure in the water.

Swimming was one of the few things that broke up the placid monotony of Tarzan's daily life, which was a slow round of searching for food, eating, and sleeping. His band roamed its own territory, separate from the territories of other nearby groups of apes. Sometimes they stayed in one area for months; at other times they traveled from the highlands down to the sea in less than a day.

Whenever they visited the shore, Tarzan found himself inexplicably fascinated by the locked and shuttered cabin on the beach. He would try to peek in the windows or down the chimney, desperately curious to know what was inside. His child's imagination filled the strange overgrown den with wonderful creatures, and the impossibility of getting inside made him want to solve the mystery even more.

The other apes stayed away from the place—the older members of the band still remembered the terrors of the gun too well and had passed on their fears to their young. Tarzan had never been told about his own connection with the cabin. The language of the apes was very limited and so was their memory; it was difficult for Kala to explain to him something so complicated and alien. She had told him only that his father had been a strange white ape. Tarzan did not know that she was not his real mother.

But in spite of that he was drawn to the cabin. And one day, when he realized that the building's door was a thing separate from its walls, he began to focus all his efforts on getting inside. He spent hours poking and prodding at the hinges, the handle, and the latch, until at last he stumbled on the right combination of motions. The door creaked open before his astonished eyes, and he leaped back, barking in surprise.

It was several minutes before he had the courage to go in. But finally, when no creatures rushed out to attack him and his eyes began to see features of the dim interior, he stepped cautiously through the doorway.

In the middle of the floor lay the skeleton of John Clayton, where Kerchak had dropped it many years ago. Another skeleton lay on the bed, and in a cradle lay yet another skeleton, a tiny one. Tarzan examined them, but, knowing they were long dead, he quickly lost interest in them. He had seen far too many dead and dying animals in his life in the jungle to be very curious about these. Death was a part of life, and the apes forgot even their own dead quickly. If he had known that he was seeing the skeletons of his own mother and father, he would not have felt much more for them.

The other things that lay in the room were far more interesting. He spent most of the day minutely examining things that he could not begin to comprehend—tools, books, paper, clothing. In the humid heat many of the things had rusted or rotted almost beyond recognition. Others crumbled to pieces at his touch.

In chests and boxes he found a few things that were better preserved, including a hunting knife with a sharp and shining blade. Grabbing it awkwardly, he cut his hand, and dropped it with a grunt of surprise. But his curiosity drew him back to it, and after a few more pricks and cuts he began to understand the bite of this strange fang. Soon he was hacking eagerly at tables and chairs, watching the splinters fly.

But at last he grew bored with chopping and began to explore further. In a small trunk he found a book filled with brightly colored pictures—a child's illustrated alphabet book that Alice had packed secretly before she left England.

> A is for Archer
> Who shoots with a bow.
> B is for Boy,
> His first name is Joe.

The pictures fascinated him. Many of them were of apes with faces like his own, and further into the book he found some of the monkeys that he saw flitting through the trees every day. But nowhere in the book were there any proper apes, with faces like his mother's or his friends'.

At first he tried to pick the figures up off the pages, but soon he realized that they weren't real. He had no idea what they might be, and no words to describe them.

The pictures of boats and trains, cows and horses, were meaningless to him, but even they were not as strange as the odd little things beneath and between them. He wondered if they were some peculiar kind of bug, since many of them had legs—although none of them seemed to have eyes or a mouth. It was Tarzan's first introduction to the letters of the alphabet.

He had never seen print before, had never even spoken with any living creature that had the remotest idea that such a thing as written language existed. He couldn't begin to imagine what a unique tool he held in his hands.

But still the pictures held his attention for hours. He went through the pages again and again. He found Sabor, the lioness, and Histah, the snake, and other things that seemed like creatures he knew, but were not. He had never enjoyed anything as much as this. He sat with the book until it started to get dark and the pictures began to blur on the pages.

Then he put the book back in the trunk and closed the lid so that no one else would find his treasure and destroy it. As he started out of the cabin he noticed the knife lying where he had dropped it. He picked it up again, thinking that this strange tooth would be something to show his friends. He left the cabin and shut the door carefully behind him.

As he moved away from the cabin his sensitive ears caught the sound of other creatures nearby. Peering through the dusk, he saw a strange band of apes drinking at the stream that flowed down to the sea. "Hu," he murmured, suddenly wary. He crept toward the jungle's edge. These apes were of a breed that was larger and more aggressive than his own, and Kala had often warned him about their forays into his own band's territory, when they would attack any of his people they found alone.

But before he could reach the safety of the trees, a hulking, shadowy form came bounding toward him out of the dusk. It was the leader of the strange apes, a huge male, baring terrible, long teeth and ready to tear him apart.

The boy had no time to run before the ape was on top of him, knocking him to the ground. He screamed as its teeth sank into his shoulder, barely missing his throat. He kicked wildly with his feet and flailed with his hands—and suddenly felt the knife he still held sink into the giant ape's side. The creature roared with pain, attacking him more fiercely. Screaming, Tarzan stabbed at it again and again, pummeled it with his fists and feet, and bit it with his own useless teeth as it tore at him in a frenzy. Then his knife struck something vital. The giant ape stiffened upright above him, then collapsed across his exhausted body. Silence fell and the two forms lay motionless in the sand.

A mile back in the forest, the apes were feeding among the trees. But when the sound of a struggle reached them from the beach, Kala stopped eating with a sudden feeling of fear. She knew that Tarzan had gone off on his own to the cabin and had not returned. She dropped the leafy branch she had been gnawing and swung off through the trees to investigate.

When she reached the shore, she saw the bodies of the strange ape and her child lying side by side, unmoving. She raced across the moonlit beach to Tarzan's side, whimpering and hooting her dismay. She pulled him away from the dead ape, not able to imagine how her child could have killed such a fearsome enemy. Tarzan moaned softly, and she knew that at least he was still alive in spite of the terrible wounds all over his body. She

tried to get him to cling to her, but he was
still unconscious. After picking him up awkwardly, she carried him away into the trees.

4

Many days passed and Kala tended Tarzan in the only ways she knew how. She licked his wounds to keep them clean and brushed away the flies and other insects that buzzed constantly around him. At first he could not even eat, and lay tossing and moaning in a feverish delirium in their nest among the branches. He only wanted water, and she carried it to him held in her own mouth. No human mother could have been more unselfish and devoted than this wild creature was to the orphaned child in her keeping.

At last Tarzan's fever broke and he began to recover. Kala left him alone sometimes now so she could hunt for food to feed them both. For many days the boy kept to himself, bearing the pain of his wounds silently and privately, as wild creatures did.

In time he was able to walk again, and swim. After that he recovered his old strength and stamina quickly, although livid purple scars marked his forehead and shoulders and chest, reminders of his nearly fatal fight.

While he was recovering from his wounds, he had repeatedly gone over his battle with the huge ape and realized how the miraculous weapon he had found had saved his life. He knew that if he could get his hands on the knife again, he would no longer be a weakling. He would have protection not only against other wild animals but also against the bullying of Tublat and the bigger apes in his own band. And he also longed to go back to the cabin to explore again the things he had found there.

As soon as he was able to make the journey, he returned to the beach near the cabin. He found the bones of his attacker picked clean by scavengers, and in the skeleton he found the knife, dark with dried blood and rust. He drove the knife into the sand, shouting defiantly at the bones of his enemy. And after he had finished his display of triumph, he found his knife polished clean again.

After that he went back to the cabin, and in a few minutes he had found a way to trip the lock and get inside. He studied the latch and lock a while longer, until he began to see how they worked together. Now he could close and lock the door so that he could explore the cabin without worrying about intruders.

He went again to the chest where he had found the alphabet book and took it out. There were a few more books in the trunk, too, including some other primers, more picture books, and a dictionary. He looked through them all, finding the strange little "bugs" in all of them, but he was much more interested in the pictures. He squatted for hours on top of the table in the cabin his father had built, turning the pages of book after book with his strong, slender hands. His mother and father would never have known this wild, brown little boy as their own. He could not speak a word in any human language; he couldn't remember having ever seen another human being. And yet he was still their son, and some instinct drew him to discover for himself the legacy they would have given him.

Tarzan stared at the alphabet book in his hands, which was open to a picture of a little ape that looked very much like he did. The little ape was covered, except for its face and hands, with strange, colored fur. The fur was actually clothing, but Tarzan had never seen clothing worn before. Beneath the picture were three little bugs:

BOY

He saw that those three bugs appeared again farther down the page—and often they appeared together in the same little group he saw beneath the picture. He began to realize that there really weren't many different bugs, that the same ones simply appeared again and again, gathered into different groups.

He turned the page, looking for the combination of B-O-Y again. And there he found a picture of another little ape, standing beside something that looked like a jackal. The bugs beneath the picture were

A BOY AND HIS DOG.

"Hu!" He touched the three letters eagerly, delighting in his discovery. He had taken the first step on a long journey.

After that he spent more and more time at the cabin, poring over the books, searching for more patterns and fitting them to pictures. It was a thing any child his age in England would have taken for granted, but because he had never even heard of language or writing, he had to re-invent their rules step by step, completely on his own. It took him a very long time, and his progress was frustratingly slow. There were too many concepts he lacked the experience to understand, and he had no one he could ask about them.

During the next two years he returned to the cabin almost every day. When he was about twelve, he discovered a cache of pencils in a drawer. He quickly found that the pencils left a black mark on the tabletop. Before long he had decorated the whole table with loops and scrawls, wearing his pencil down to the wood. But as he picked up the next one he thought of something better to do with it. He had found one or two handwritten notes that hadn't moldered away and had seen the bugs on them. He began to try to copy the forms of the little bugs from his books.

He wasn't very successful at first because he held the pencil the way he held his knife, which did not make printing easy or particularly readable. But as months passed he found a better, more efficient way to hold the pencil so that he was able to copy the little bugs much more clearly. He had no idea what to call the thing he was doing, but he was learning to write.

As time passed he learned to recognize the combinations of letters that stood for the figures in his alphabet book and some of the ones in his picture books. He still had no idea what most of the pictures were, and almost no idea of the uses of verbs or adjectives or other parts of speech. But he knew all the bugs that appeared in his books and could line them up in the order they appeared in the alphabet. Eventually he discovered the order of words in the dictionary, and the words and pictures there helped him to guess at even more clues in his mystery. By the time he was seventeen, he could read.

And beyond that he had discovered something far more important. He no longer felt ashamed of his hairless body or his odd features, because he had learned from the pictures that he was a different kind of creature from the other members of his band. They were A-P-E-S, just as old Sabor was a L-I-O-N-E-S-S and Histah a S-N-A-K-E. And he—he was a M-A-N.

There were many interruptions in Tarzan's studies because of the wanderings of his band; but even when he was far from the cabin, he continued to scratch out words with his knife point on branches and bark.

As he explored the mysterious clues of his lost heritage, Tarzan kept working to improve the skills that had helped him survive in the wild. He practiced his tracking and hunting, as well as his swimming and rope throwing. He found new uses for his knife as well, and learned to keep it sharp by whetting it on flat stones.

The band had grown larger since Tarzan was a baby. Under Kerchak's ruthless leadership they had been able to frighten other competing bands from their part of the jungle, so they had plenty to eat and little fear of predators. More young males stayed with the band, or brought new mates back to it, to live peacefully under Kerchak's rule instead of trying to start new bands of their own. The younger males rarely tried to challenge Kerchak's leadership, knowing his ferocious strength too well.

Tarzan's position in the band was a peculiar one. The others considered him one of them, yet they knew he was different and unpredictable. The older males either ignored him entirely or else hated him so much that, except for his quickness and agility and the fierce protection of Kala, he might have been killed long ago.

Tublat was his worst enemy. But it was because of Tublat, when Tarzan was about thirteen, that the boy's persecution by the others finally stopped and he was left almost completely alone.

On the night that Tarzan earned his right to respect, the apes had gathered in a small natural amphitheater. The night was clear and a full moon hung in the sky overhead, shedding its silver light on the band's activities.

As the apes gathered leafy branches and piled them in the crooks of sturdy trees to make nests for the night, the moon's light began to dim. Looking up, they saw that it was not the trees that obscured the moon, or even clouds. The moon was simply disappearing. It was disappearing into the earth's shadow in a lunar eclipse, but to the apes it seemed that the shining orb was being swallowed up forever.

The apes stopped their nest building and began to gather in the open space in the center of the clearing, looking up, panting and grunting querulously. As the moon's face continued to disappear, the hooting and restless stirring of the apes grew. Some picked up branches and shook them at the sky. Tarzan watched in awe, crouching beside Kala; not even in his books had he seen anything so strange and terrifying.

Some of the apes began to pound their branches on a hollow log in the clearing. A dull, rhythmic booming rang through the forest, startling the jungle creatures as they hunted or slept. Other apes began to leap and call, swinging wildly through the trees. The apes tried, in their primitive way, to call back the moon; to find some way in which they could influence and control the vast, mysterious universe that surrounded them—just as Tarzan's own prehistoric human ancestors had done far back in the dawn of time. And soon

Tarzan was part of the wild, leaping horde as their dance spoke to something deep inside him. His slim, sweat-streaked body whirled gracefully among the heavy, leaping apes, and he shouted at the moon with mingled exuberance and fear.

But when it seemed that their actions were futile, the apes only became more frenzied, until their wild display went out of control. Kerchak sprang into the open space by the hollow log, then threw back his head to roar a challenge at the sky while he beat his chest. And then he lunged after the nearest ape and tore at her side with his cruel teeth. She screamed and leaped away as he turned, in a rage, to attack another ape. Other females gathered up their infants and fled, as they had on a night long ago. Younger apes scrambled for the shelter of the trees as more and more of the older males caught Kerchak's moon madness and began to fight.

Tublat, who had been enviously watching Tarzan's lithe, graceful dance in the clearing, suddenly rushed toward him, jaws open. In Tublat's twisted thoughts, the ugly, hairless young ape was to blame for the strange disappearance of the moon.

Tarzan saw his old enemy coming, and he leaped away after the females and young, hoping to hide among them. But Tublat was so close on his heels that Tarzan realized he would be lucky to escape at all. He leaped up and caught the lowest limb of a tree, then clambered up into its branches, with Tublat following. Tarzan quickly reached the very top of the tree and perched safely among branches that were too small to hold Tublat's weight. Tarzan hooted and threw taunts at his enemy, who crouched fifty feet below him, glaring furiously upward. Just then the moon disappeared completely.

And Tublat went completely mad.

Roaring and shrieking his rage, he dropped back to the ground and ran at the scurrying females and their young, then sank his teeth into a dozen tiny necks and tore at the backs and shoulders of the females who tried to stop him.

Tarzan could barely see Tublat's attack from his treetop, but he heard the females and their young fleeing frantically through the trees. Even the other male apes ran from Tublat's lunatic frenzy into the deepest shadows of the night.

And then Tarzan recognized the one ape who had not quite reached safety. At the same moment Tublat saw her and rushed to attack. It was Kala, and seeing her, Tarzan dropped down through the branches like a falling stone.

Kala leaped to catch an overhanging branch, with Tublat close behind. She should have been safe, but the branch broke beneath her weight with a ripping crack and she fell back on top of him, knocking him to the ground.

Both of them were up in an instant, but as Kala turned to face Tublat's attack she found Tarzan standing between her and her infuriated mate.

Nothing could have suited Tublat better. He sprang at the boy with a snarl. But his teeth never closed on that small, hairless body.

Tarzan's strong young hand caught Tublat by the throat, and he plunged his keen hunting knife a dozen times into Tublat's chest. He struck as quickly as lightning and only stopped when he felt Tublat begin to crumple.

As the body rolled to the ground a glimmer of light fell across it through the trees. The boy looked up and saw the moon begin to reappear from the darkness. Tarzan of the Apes threw back his fierce young head and gave a wild cry of triumph.

One by one the members of the band swung down or crept out from their hiding places and formed a circle around Tarzan and his vanquished foe. When they had all gathered, Tarzan looked from one to another.

"I am Tarzan!" he cried. "I am a great killer. No one will touch Tarzan of the Apes or his mother, Kala, again. See how I have brought back the moon. None of you are as mighty as Tarzan. Let his enemies remember."

Looking directly at Kerchak, whose eyes were still dim with the aftereffects of his rage, Tarzan struck his chest and shouted his defiance again.

5

The next day the band started to move slowly back through the jungle, toward the coast again. Once Sabor, the lioness, crossing their path, sent them scurrying into the safety of the tall trees. She respected their numbers and their strength, but they held her fangs and her ferocity in equal respect. Only Tarzan, crouching on a low-hanging branch, dared to fling down a nut so that it struck her sharply between the ears. The lioness stopped, looking up with smoldering eyes at the taunting figure above her. She laid back her ears, baring her fangs in a snarl that warned him she would never forget this insult. She roared loudly, lashing her tail, and Tarzan gave his own cry of defiance from the safety of the tree. He had never forgotten how she had killed his cousin and almost killed him. Indeed, she had killed far too many unwary young apes, and he longed for some way to rid the band of her threat, but he knew that he was far too weak to fight her face-to-face.

For a moment the two eyed each other in silence, and then the great cat turned away and disappeared into the jungle. Tarzan continued to stare at the spot where Sabor had stood while strange new thoughts rolled over and over in his head. He had killed Tublat. He was a mighty fighter. There must be some way he could track down the lioness and kill her too. Then he would be the mightiest hunter in the band. And then he could take Sabor's beautiful skin and wear it for his own.

In his books he had learned the difference between *man* and *ape*. He had seen that *man* hunted other creatures and took their skins to cover his own. Man called these skins *clothes*. When he was younger, Tarzan had wished that he could have the skin of Sabor, the lioness, or Sheeta, the leopard, to cover his hairless body so that he would look more like an ape. Then he became proud of his hairless skin because he had learned that it was proof that he belonged to a people even greater than the apes. He had been happy to go naked, showing all the jungle his ancestry.

Yet the men he saw in pictures covered themselves with artificial skins. He wondered why. Surely they must be as proud to be superior to other creatures as he was. It was a question he hadn't been able to answer. Moving slowly through the jungle, eating figs and insects, he still could not decide what clothes meant to men.

But before long he had other, more important things to think about. The jungle was growing darker and darker as storm clouds hid the sun high above the ceiling of green branches. The jungle noises ceased; the trees stood still as though in paralyzed anticipation of some imminent disaster. All nature waited—but not for long.

Faintly, from a distance, came a low, sad moaning. It came nearer, growing louder and louder. The great trees bent in unison as though pressed down by a mighty hand. Closer and closer to the ground they bowed, and still there was no sound but the deep moaning of the wind.

Then suddenly the giant trees whipped back, lashing their mighty tops in angry, deafening protest. A vivid, blinding stroke of lightning dazzled the darkness of the black clouds sweeping overhead. Thunder boomed like cannon fire. The deluge came, inundating the jungle.

The ape band huddled at the bases of the great trees, shivering in the cold rain. Flashes of lightning illuminated wildly waving branches, whipping streamers of water, and bending trunks. At times some gigantic ancient tree, struck by lightning, would crash into a thousand pieces in the surrounding woods, carrying down numberless branches and smaller trees to the tangled confusion of the jungle floor.

Branches, torn off by the wind, fell through the wild, blowing darkness to crush the hapless creatures who crowded the thickly inhabited world below. For hours the storm's fury continued, and the band huddled close together in fear. They held palm leaves over their heads, panting and hooting their discomfort at the pitiless elements.

At last the storm passed, as suddenly as it had begun. The wind died, the sun broke through—Nature smiled once more. The dripping leaves and branches, the moist petals of flowers in all the colors of the rainbow, glistened in the beauty of the returning day. As Nature forgot, her children forgot also. Life picked up and went on as it had before.

But during the misery of the storm a new thought had come to Tarzan. Suddenly he understood the mystery of clothes. How much more snug and comfortable he would have been under Sabor's heavy coat! Now he saw that his own people were wise in more ways than he had imagined.

For several months the band foraged near the beach, and Tarzan spent most of his time in the cabin, studying. But whenever he moved through the forest, he kept a loop of vine ready at his side, and he captured many small, unwary animals in its noose. In his mind a new plan was forming.

Once he dropped the noose over the neck of a wild boar, and its mad lunge for freedom jerked the boy down from the overhanging branch where he had been lying in wait. The boar turned at the sound of his fall and, seeing only the easy prey of a young ape, lowered its head and charged.

Luckily Tarzan was only winded, uninjured by the fall. He scrambled to his feet as the boar charged, and leaped back up into the safety of the branches. He had lost a long rope and learned the hard way about the limits of his special weapon. If it had been Sabor who had dragged him down, the outcome of his accident might have been far worse.

It took him many days to find another vine of the right sort, long and strong enough for his needs. But when it was finished, he lay in wait with it in the branches of a tree above a well-traveled path that led to a waterhole. Several small animals passed below, and he let them go. He was interested in only one prey.

At last the one he had waited for came padding noiselessly along the trail, her muscles flowing sinuously beneath her glossy hide: Sabor, the lioness. Her head was high and alert. Her tail moved in a graceful, constant undulation. She came closer and closer to where Tarzan waited, the coils of rope ready in his hand.

Tarzan sat like a statue of bronze as Sabor

passed beneath him. And then his silent loop shot out at her.

For an instant the noose hung in the air like a great snake. And then Sabor looked up, hearing its faint hiss, and it settled around her neck. With a quick jerk Tarzan pulled the noose tight and then let go of the rope, clinging to his branch with both hands.

Sabor bounded away into the jungle; but Tarzan had learned from his mistake with the boar. This time he had tied the rope securely to the trunk of the tree. The lioness had taken half of a second bound when her body flipped completely over in the air and she fell on her back with a heavy crash.

So far Tarzan's plan had worked perfectly. But when it came to hauling the struggling, clawing, biting, screaming mass of iron-muscled lioness up the tree and into the air, he found that he had taken on too much. Sabor's weight was tremendous, and when she braced her paws, nothing short of Tantor, the elephant, could have budged her.

The lioness was now back on the path, and she could see clearly who had caused her this indignity. Roaring with rage, she suddenly charged, leaping for the limb where Tarzan stood. But when she reached it, he was no longer there. He balanced on a smaller branch twenty feet overhead, dancing and mocking her, throwing down twigs and branches. At last she dropped to the earth again, and Tarzan climbed down to seize the rope. But Sabor had discovered that it was only a vine that held her, and she chewed it in two with her powerful jaws before Tarzan could pull it tight again.

Tarzan shouted and grimaced with disappointment and defiance. His well-laid plan had failed, and all he could do now was make useless noises at the roaring beast below him.

Sabor paced back and forth beneath the tree for hours. Four times she crouched and sprang at the dancing boy, but always he seemed to melt away before she could reach him, as elusive as the wind.

At last Tarzan grew tired of baiting her. He hurled a piece of fruit down at her head and swung off through the trees to rejoin his band.

He told them of his adventure, swelling his chest and gesturing so boldly that even his

worst enemies were impressed, and Kala
groomed him fondly, grunting her satisfaction. Even her child's defeats were remarkable.

6

The years passed but little changed for Tarzan in his wild existence. He grew stronger and more experienced in the ways of the jungle, and he learned from his books more strange bits of half-understood lore about the world that lay somewhere outside his primeval forest.

His life was satisfying to him most of the time. There were always fish to be caught in the many streams and lakes, jokes to be played with friends, the cabin by the shore, and Sabor, with all her ferocious relatives, to keep him alert and give him moments of excitement. He taunted but no longer hunted the lioness, having thought of no new foolproof plan; but big cats often hunted him. And though they never quite reached him with their cruel, sharp claws, there were often times when they came within a leaf's thickness of it. The lioness and the leopard were quick, but Tarzan of the Apes was lightning.

Tarzan made friends with Tantor, the elephant. How he did it was their secret, which he never shared with anyone. But on many moonlit nights the boy and the great bull elephant walked the jungle trails together, and where the way was clear, Tarzan rode high on Tantor's mighty back.

He still spent much time in his parents' cabin, where their bones lay, untouched, along with the skeleton of Kala's baby. At eighteen, he had read and reread all of the books he could find, although his understanding of what he read was limited by the narrowness of his own experience, and filled with fantastic half-truths that seemed as reasonable to him as the reality would have. He could also write, in a limited way, printing letters quickly and plainly to make simple sentences.

At eighteen the young English lord could speak no English, even though he read and wrote it marginally. He had still never seen another human being in his ape band's small corner of the jungle world.

But one day, as he sat poring over one of his parents' books, the ancient security of his jungle was being broken forever.

At the far eastern edge of the band's territory, a strange line of figures was moving in single file along a hidden animal trail. At its head was a group of warriors armed with slender wooden spears and long bows with poisoned arrows. On their backs were oval shields decorated with bright geometric images. Their faces and chests were tattooed with more geometric designs, each warrior's as different as his own features, and they wore many strands of copper and glass beads around their necks and arms.

Following them were several hundred women and children, carrying with them all the worldly goods they would need to establish a new village and a new life in this unexplored territory. In the rear another group of warriors guarded their passage.

The rear guard was larger than the advance party—these natives felt they had less to fear from the unknown than from the place they were fleeing. The soldiers of the colonial government had harassed them and mistreated them so much in their endless search for rubber and ivory that the natives had finally fought back, killing a white officer and a small detachment of his black troops.

They had thought that would mean an end to their persecution, but they were mistaken. The colonial government had sent out a larger body of troops, which had attacked their village, killing many of their people. The survivors had fled into the jungle, heading into the unknown and what they hoped would be freedom.

For three days the villagers traveled through the trackless jungle, until finally, early on the fourth day, they came to a spot on the banks of a small river, which seemed to be the best place they had seen for building a new home.

They began the work of constructing their new village, and in a month a great clearing had been cut in the jungle. Soon huts and walls were erected, and plantains and yams started to grow in gardens. Before long they were living their old life in their new home. Here there were no Europeans, no soldiers, no rubber or ivory to be gathered for cruel and thankless taskmasters.

Several more months passed before any hunters needed to venture far from the village in search of game. But one day Kulonga, son of the village headman, wandered far into the dense forests to the west of the village. He moved warily, his spear held ready, his bow at his back, and many slim, straight arrows smeared with tarry poison in his quiver.

When darkness fell he was far from the palisades of his father's village, so he climbed into the fork of a large tree and slept there for the night.

Not much farther west slept Kerchak's band of apes.

Early the next morning the apes started out into the jungle to search for food. Tarzan went off, as he usually did, toward the cabin on the beach, filling his stomach with fruit and nuts he found along the way. The apes scattered in all directions, always staying within the sound of an alarm.

Kala had moved slowly along an elephant track toward the east and was turning over rotted branches and logs, searching for succulent insects, when she heard the faintest shadow of a noise. She looked along the trail, which ran straight ahead of her, and saw a strange and frightening creature coming toward her down the leafy tunnel.

It was Kulonga.

Kala didn't wait to see more. She turned, moving rapidly back along the trail. She did not run, for something about the strange creature was oddly familiar; but she wanted to avoid any closer contact.

Kulonga ran after her, seeing only an animal, the meat he had been hunting for all this time. This huge creature could feed his relatives and friends for many days. He drew back his arm and hurled his spear.

The spear grazed Kala's side. She gave a cry of rage and pain, turning on her tormentor. In an instant the sound of other apes hurrying to her rescue filled the jungle.

As Kala charged, Kulonga unslung his bow and fitted an arrow to the string. He drew it quickly and sent the poisoned shaft straight into Kala's heart.

With a terrible scream, Kala plunged forward and fell dead before the astonished eyes of the rest of her band.

The apes rushed toward her killer, but he was already running off down the trail as swiftly as a frightened antelope. Racing through the trees, they followed him a long way; but finally, one by one, they gave up the chase and returned to Kala's body. Tarzan was the only man they had ever seen before, and they could only wonder fearfully what sort of strange creature had invaded their jungle.

Far away, on the beach by the cabin, Tarzan heard faint echoes of the apes' distress calls. Realizing that something was seriously wrong, he hurried back to find the rest of the band.

When he arrived, he found them gathered around the body of his mother, screeching and wailing their unhappiness. Tarzan stared at his mother's motionless form. More grief and anger than he had ever known filled him as he crouched beside her, hearing the other apes tell how a creature they had never seen before had mysteriously struck her down. Tarzan pulled at his mother's body, trying to lift her, trying to make her move again. But her deep brown eyes did not open to look at him, and he knew they never would again.

He flung himself down across her body and began to sob, as he had not done since he was an infant. He had lost the only being in the entire world who had shown him affection and love, and it was the greatest tragedy he had ever known.

It did not matter that Kala was only an ape. To Tarzan she had been kind, she had been beautiful. He had felt all the love for her that any human child could feel for his mother; and she had loved him as much in her way as Lady Alice would have if she had lived.

After his first outburst of grief, Tarzan was able to control himself enough to question the other members of the band about the killing. They told him all they could with their limited vocabulary.

It was enough to tell him what he needed to know: that a strange, hairless black ape with bright-colored feathers growing from its body had somehow thrown a twig that killed Kala, and then had run away down the track.

Tarzan got to his feet and leaped up into the branches of a tree, leaving the apes. Only one thing mattered to him now—to find the creature who had killed his mother and avenge her death. He knew the windings of the elephant trail that Kala's murderer had taken, and so he cut straight through the jungle to intercept him.

After an hour he struck the trail again and came down from the trees to search it for tracks. In the soft mud on the bank of a tiny stream he found footprints that he recognized. Only one other creature in all the jungle made prints like that—Tarzan himself. Could it be that he was trailing a man— one of his own kind?

There were two sets of prints going in opposite directions. His quarry had already returned past this point. But the tracks were very fresh; he could not be far ahead. Tarzan swung up into the trees again and traveled swiftly and noiselessly above the trail.

He had barely gone a mile when he found the mysterious creature standing in a small open space. The hunter held his slender bow in one hand and was fitting an arrow to its string. On the other side of the clearing stood a wild boar. Head lowered, foam flecking its tusks, it was ready to charge.

Tarzan looked down on the strange being in wonder—a man, so much like he was, only different in color. How much more impressive it was to see a man in the flesh rather than just in the dull, printed pictures of a book! The hunter drew his bow and suddenly his pose was so familiar that Tarzan almost called out, giving himself away.

A is for Archer.

This was an archer, like the one in his alphabet book. Tarzan watched him draw his arrow far back and then release it as the boar charged. It flew with the speed of thought and lodged in the boar's bristling neck.

The arrow had barely left his bow before Kulonga had fitted another to it; but the boar was on him before he could fire. The hunter leaped high over the back of the attacking beast and, turning with incredible speed, planted a second arrow in the boar's back. Then he leaped up into the branches of a tree.

The boar wheeled to charge his enemy one more time; he took a dozen steps, then staggered and fell on his side. For a moment he thrashed convulsively. Then he lay still.

Kulonga came down from the tree. Using the knife that hung at his side, he cut several large pieces of meat from the boar's body. He built a fire in the middle of the clearing, then cooked and ate his fill. Then he smothered the fire, took the rest of his meat with him, and set off into the jungle.

Tarzan watched his activities with fascination. The thought of revenge still burned brightly inside him, but his desire to learn was even stronger. He decided to follow the archer and find out where he came from. Tarzan knew that he could kill him easily enough, any time he chose.

When Kulonga had left the clearing, Tarzan dropped quietly to the ground. He cut strips of meat from the boar's carcass and ate them raw. He had seen fire, but only when lightning struck some great tree. That any creature could produce the red and yellow fangs that devoured wood and left nothing but dust amazed him. He was even more surprised that the archer had ruined his delicious fresh meat by throwing it into the fire before he ate it. He touched the still-warm coals, snatching away his hand as the hidden fire burned him. He wondered vaguely whether the fire was a friend that the archer was sharing his food with. Whatever his reasons had been, Tarzan had no intention of ruining his own meat that way. After he had eaten, he buried the rest of the carcass where he could find it later.

And then Lord Greystoke wiped his greasy fingers on his thighs and continued his pursuit. All day he followed Kulonga, hovering over him in the trees like a malign spirit. Twice more he saw the archer use his arrows on other creatures—once a hyena and once an antelope. Each time the animal died almost instantly. Kulonga's poison was very fresh and very deadly.

Tarzan thought a great deal about this remarkable new way of hunting as he followed his quarry along the trail. He knew that just the bite of the arrow could not be enough to kill these wild things of the jungle, who were often wounded terribly when they fought each other, but recovered as often as not. He knew there must be some special mystery connected with these tiny slivers of wood that could kill with a scratch.

That night Kulonga slept in the crotch of a mighty tree, and Tarzan of the Apes crouched high above him in its branches, waiting.

When Kulonga woke in the morning, he found that his bow and arrows had disappeared. More frightened than angry, he searched the tree and the ground below it, but there was no sign of either the bow and arrows or whatever had stolen them.

Kulonga was panic-stricken. Had he offended some spirit of the forest? He had lost his spear when he had thrown it at the ape, and now his bow and arrows were gone. He was defenseless, except for his knife; his only hope lay in reaching his village as quickly as possible. He was sure that he was not far from it now, and he took the trail as quickly as he could.

Tarzan swung along quietly above him. Kulonga's bow and arrows hung securely in a tree behind him, ready to be picked up on his return journey.

The youth was almost directly above Kulonga's head when the hunter reached his destination at last. Here the forest ended abruptly, and just beyond the trees lay planted fields and the walls of the village. Tarzan felt fresh anger fill him as he again thought of Kala's death. He had to act quickly or his quarry would escape.

Quick action was something the jungle had taught him long ago, just as it had taught him the harsh justice of an eye for an eye. He dropped rapidly down through the branches of the tree, landing on top of the unsuspecting hunter and knocking him to the ground. Before the other could even struggle, Tarzan had plunged his knife into the man's chest. Kala was avenged.

Tarzan stood looking down at the dead man's body and his anger slowly cooled. Once a thing was done, the creatures of the jungle did not dwell on it. Instead he examined the hunter's body carefully. He removed the hunter's knife and its sheath. He admired the tattooing on the dead man's forehead and chest and took the decorative breastplate of bone and bright parrot feathers for himself. He also took the breechcloth, made from soft hide—the *clothes* that all proper *men* wore—and a copper anklet that appealed to him.

He did not feel guilty or ashamed at taking the belongings from the man he had just killed. He had read books, but he had never lived among the people who had written them or been raised to obey or understand the laws of civilized society. He had survived by the law of the jungle all his life, a wild thing whose habits had far more in common with apes and lions than with human beings. The law of the jungle was the only law he knew.

And the law he knew told him that, having killed this creature, he could also eat its meat. He was hungry and he raised his knife, ready to cut into its flesh.

But then he hesitated. He had killed Tublat, whom he had hated and who had hated him; but he had never considered eating Tublat's flesh. Apes did not eat other apes—it was equal to cannibalism, if he had known what that was. But who was this being, that he could not be eaten like any of the wild things that preyed on each other to eat and live?

A strange doubt stopped Tarzan. His books had taught him that he was a man, even though he had always lived as an ape. Did men eat men? He had no idea. Yet he could not bring down his knife. All he knew was that he could not eat the flesh of this man, whose form was more like his own than any ape's.

Leaving Kulonga's body where it lay, he swung back into the trees.

7

Tarzan quickly found a spot where the forest's edge came right up to the walls of the village. Driven by a burning need to see more creatures of his own kind and to learn how they lived, he peered down over the log wall from the safety of an immense tree overhung with thick foliage and creepers.

He watched with wonder from his hidden place among the leaves and vines, taking in every feature of this strange new world. There were naked children running and playing like young apes among the village huts. There were women grinding dried plantains in stone mortars while others made cakes from the powdered flour. Out in the fields he could see other women hoeing, weeding, and gathering. The women wore skirts of woven dried grass, and many wore masses of brass and copper bracelets and anklets or wide collars of beads and coiled wire.

Tarzan watched them with growing curiosity. There seemed to be only a few men in the village. Could the others be out hunting? A few of the men who remained stood guard at the edges of the forest while the rest dozed in the shade of their huts. None of the men tilled the fields or performed any of the daily activities of the village. This surprised him, since among the apes both males and females did the same things in their day-to-day lives, except that the females also cared for the young.

Tarzan watched a woman working directly beneath him, where a small caldron bubbled over a fire. On the ground to one side lay a handful of wooden arrows. These she dipped into the thick, reddish tar bubbling in the pot and then laid on a rack of boughs. Tarzan was fascinated. He saw how careful the woman was not to touch the red tar, and he realized that this must be the secret of the deadly effectiveness of the arrows. He knew little about poison—only that he must never eat certain plants—but he sensed that the arrow was only a kind of messenger that carried the poison into a victim's body.

He wished that he could get his hands on more of those deadly slivers, wished that the woman would leave her work for a moment so that he could drop down and take a handful. As he was trying to think of some way to distract her, one of the sentries gave a cry from across the field. The body of Kala's murderer, Kulonga, had been discovered. Almost everyone in the village, including the woman below him, rushed toward the village gate and out into the fields.

Silently Tarzan dropped to the ground beside the caldron of poison. He stood tensely for a moment, his quick, bright eyes searching the compound. No one was in sight. He looked toward the open doorway of a nearby hut and curiosity overcame his caution. He moved slowly toward the low, thatched building. He stopped at the door, listening intently. When he was sure there was no one inside, he slipped into the shadowy interior.

Weapons hung on the walls—long spears, strangely shaped knives, narrow shields. In the center of the room was a fire pit, and at the far end were beds made of dry grasses covered by woven mats. Several clay pots sat near the fire.

Tarzan hefted the spears, and wanted to take one, but decided that he could not carry it and the arrows too. Then he investigated everything in the room, placing each object in a pile by the fireplace. He topped the pile with an inverted pot, like a head, and draped Kulonga's feather-and-bone breastplate below it. Then he stood back, grinning his satisfaction; he, like his ape friends, loved pranks and mischief.

The next moment he heard the villagers returning, wailing and lamenting their grief. Startled, he ran to the doorway and looked toward the gate. No one was in sight yet, but he knew that they would be very soon.

He darted outside to the pile of arrows. Gathering up all he could carry, he pushed over the caldron and clambered back up the wall into the waiting trees. He hid among the branches again, waiting and watching.

The villagers entered the gate, four of them carrying the dead body of Kulonga. They brought it to the doorway of the hut that Tarzan had just visited. The men carried the body inside—and came hurrying out again, with exclamations of amazement and fear. The other villagers gathered around the doorway; several warriors entered the hut again, armed with spears.

Finally an old man, wearing many ornaments and carrying the ritual fly whisk of zebra's tail that meant he was the village headman, entered the hut. He was Mbonga, the father of Kulonga. For a few moments everyone was silent. Then Mbonga emerged from the hut again, wearing an expression of mingled rage and awe. He spoke a few words to the waiting warriors, and then they were off, searching every hut and corner of the village.

Someone else discovered the overturned caldron and the stolen arrows. The rest of the villagers gathered around their headman, their voices rising in fear. To find Kulonga dead so close to their village was terrible enough—but to find his own hut ransacked, within the safety of the village walls, surely meant that some angry spirit was at work. The villagers glanced around them as they spoke, feeling as though hidden eyes were watching.

And hidden eyes were. Tarzan watched them for a long time from his hiding place, unable to tear himself away. Much of their behavior was meaningless to him because he understood almost nothing about human beliefs and superstition and little more about fear of the unknown. But still it fascinated him.

The sun was high in the heavens when he finally turned away. He had not eaten since the day before, and it was a long way back to the place where he had left the remains of the boar. So Tarzan turned his back on the frightened village and melted away into the safety of the jungle.

8

Tarzan returned to the ape band the next day, bringing boar meat and his new bow and arrows. He told the others about his revenge and his adventures, and the apes hooted and poked curiously at the strange things he carried and now wore on his body. But Kerchak, still the leader of the band after so many years, grunted and turned away, more envious and suspicious than ever of this strange member of his band. He began to wonder whether there was some way to get rid of Tarzan now that Kala was gone.

Tarzan began to practice with his bow as soon as he could. At first he lost nearly every arrow he shot. But after a while he began to aim more accurately, and by the time a month had passed he was a fair shot with the bow. Unfortunately his practice had cost him nearly all his arrows.

The band continued to spend most of its time near the beach, so Tarzan divided his time between archery practice and studying his small store of books. And one day, exploring the cabin more carefully than he ever had before, he found a small metal box hidden in the back of a cupboard. In it was a golden locket on a chain. The locket came open in his hands, and inside it were the photographs of a smooth-faced young man and a woman with long, pale hair. There were also a few letters and a small book. Tarzan studied them all minutely.

He liked the locket best, with its smiling, open faces—the faces, though he could not know, of his mother and father. Pleased with it, he put the chain over his head, imitating the villagers he had seen who wore ornaments.

He could barely make out anything in the letters because he had never learned to read script, and the book was a complete mystery. It was full of the same little bugs, but in combinations that were completely strange. It was his father's diary, written entirely in

French. Tarzan had no idea that there were more languages than one; all he knew was that none of the words in the book appeared in his dictionary.

He also had no idea that this small book held the key to his own history, the answer to the strange riddle of his life. Frustrated, he put the book and the letters back in the box for another day. But in the meantime he had more important things to tend to. He had few arrows left. He would have to return to the village of men and steal some more.

Tarzan set out early the next morning and, traveling quickly, reached the village by afternoon. Once more he hid in the overgrown tree, watching the woman who worked at the bubbling caldron of poison directly beneath him.

For hours he waited for a chance to drop down unseen and steal some of the arrows; but nothing unusual happened to call the villagers away from their daily work. Finally the women returned from the fields and hunters emerged from the forest. When they were all inside, the gate was closed and barred. Women began to cook the evening meal, baking cakes of plantain and cooking casaba stew.

But as the evening shadows began to lengthen, Tarzan heard a shout from across the fields. A party of hunters was returning late, and they were bringing a struggling animal with them. As they neared the compound the gates were thrown open and the villagers began to shout their excitement. Then Tarzan saw the reason for their excitement—the captured animal was a man.

Struggling, he was dragged into the village, where women and children began to strike him with sticks and stones. Tarzan, wild creature of the jungle, had no way of knowing that the captive was one of the enemy who had driven these people from their original home. He would have understood their desire for revenge—but he wondered at the cruel brutality that it brought out in them. The creatures that he knew killed quickly, not by inches, as these villagers were doing.

He had been able to learn very little about the behavior of his own people from the books he had read. When he had followed

Kulonga through the forest, he had expected to find a city of strange houses on wheels, puffing clouds of black smoke from a burning tree stuck in the roof of one of them—or a sea covered with mighty floating buildings, which he had learned were called ships. He had been rather disappointed by the clay and thatch huts of the actual village, which were no more remarkable than his own cabin on the beach.

And now he began to think that his own people were far worse than apes. The villagers had tied their captive to a post, and the warriors began to stab at him with their spears, wounding him everywhere, while the others shouted and jeered. It reminded Tarzan of the murderous fits that overtook Kerchak and some of the other big male apes when some wild display of nature's fury drove them to madness. But he could see no reason for the madness he witnessed here.

He had no real desire to go on watching the ugly spectacle in the center of the village. But suddenly he noticed that it had given him his opportunity to steal more arrows. The youth dropped lightly to the soft earth by the palisade wall. He gathered up all the arrows he found there, then tied them into a bundle with a piece of vine. But as he was turning to leave he suddenly thought of the spears he had seen in the hut when he was last there. After tossing his bundle of arrows over the wall, Tarzan slipped through the shadows to the hut he had entered the last time. It was completely dark inside, but his groping hands soon found the thing he was looking for, and he started back toward the door.

He had taken only a step or two when his sharp ears heard someone approaching. He drew back silently against the far wall, drawing his knife. A moment later a woman's figure darkened the entrance. She came to the center of the hut, feeling around with her hands on the floor. Whatever she was looking for was not in its usual place; she stood up and began to search along the wall, closer and closer to the place where Tarzan stood. He raised his knife, holding his breath. And then the woman moved away again. He heard her soft exclamation as she found what she had been looking for. Then she left the hut.

He slipped to the doorway when she was gone, looking out to be certain no one else was near. And then, carrying a spear, he crept back to the wall, stopping to overturn the caldron full of poison again before he leaped like a cat into the overhanging branches of a tree.

Standing safely on a limb, he looked back through the leaves at the place where the villagers' captive now hung motionless from the stake. Suddenly, filled with an urge that he didn't really understand, Tarzan hurled the spear. It landed upright in the dirt before the stake, quivering there while the people shouted and scattered. And then Tarzan gave the eerie, challenging scream of a great ape before he swung away through the trees, leaving the villagers in frightened confusion behind him.

After they discovered the missing arrows and the overturned caldron, the villagers were certain that they had offended some spirit of their new home, perhaps by settling in this place without its permission. From then on they put out an offering of food and arrows every day at the spot where the arrows had disappeared, in the hope of appeasing the spirit if it returned again.

Meanwhile, Tarzan was making his way back to the ape band, eager to return to creatures he understood. That night he slept in the forest, then continued on his way at dawn, hunting as he traveled. All he found were a few berries and an occasional grub. He became so intent on his search for food that he forgot his usual caution. Then suddenly, looking up from a log he had been rooting under, he saw Sabor, the lioness, standing in the center of the trail, not twenty paces away.

Her yellow eyes gleamed balefully. She licked her lips as she crouched, then crept toward him with her belly flattened against the ground.

Tarzan didn't try to escape. He had been hoping for this opportunity for weeks, ever since he had gotten his new bow. Now he unslung it quickly and fitted an arrow to the string. As Sabor sprang the arrow met her in midair. At the same time Tarzan leaped aside and sent another poison-tipped arrow into the lioness's flank as she landed beyond him.

She turned with a roar and charged him again, only to be struck in the chest by a third arrow. But this time she was too close to the boy for him to get out of her way.

Tarzan went down beneath the lioness's heavy body, his knife striking home as he fell. He lay stunned for a moment beneath her, before he realized that the dead weight lying on top of him would never rise again to injure any ape or man.

He struggled out from under the great bulk of the lioness's body and got to his feet, looking down exultantly. And then he put a foot on the body of his longtime enemy, and his cry of triumph echoed through the jungle again, until all its creatures were silent, listening.

Lion meat was not usual fare for an ape, but Tarzan ate enough to ease his hunger a little. He was far happier to have Sabor's hide—the thing he had dreamed of possessing for years. It would make him the finest of clothes. He removed her pelt and rolled it up, then went on his way again.

When he reached the tribe at last, he proudly showed them the lioness's skin.

"Look!" he cried. "Apes of Kerchak. See what Tarzan the mighty hunter has done. I have killed your worst enemy. Never again will Sabor steal young apes and eat them. Who else has ever done such a thing? Tarzan is the best among you because Tarzan is not an ape. Tarzan is . . ." He broke off because the apes had no word for "man" and Tarzan could not pronounce the word in English.

The apes gathered around, touching and sniffing the lion skin, hooting their wonder at what Tarzan had done. But Tarzan turned away, suddenly no longer proud, but confused. Why couldn't he say what he was? He had so many thoughts that he had never been able to share with the other apes, even Kala. Somehow he was sure there must be something more, some way to express those things.

But then he heard Kerchak's threatening growl and, looking up, he forgot everything else.

9

As the apes of his band gathered in admiration around Tarzan, old Kerchak looked at the lion skin that Tarzan had laid out on the ground. Then he looked at Tarzan, that strange, puny creature with his stranger actions, who had never belonged here, who should never have been allowed to live—and who was claiming now that he was mightier than any ape, even Kerchak! Suddenly something snapped in Kerchak's brain. He leaped forward, roaring a challenge, striking left and right to drive the other apes away.

Tarzan leaped up into a tree, along with the others who fled Kerchak's unexpected fury. Kerchak looked up at Tarzan and roared his challenge again, daring him to come down and fight.

Tarzan dropped quickly to the ground. The other apes watched, grunting with nervous anticipation as their huge silver-backed leader charged at the lithe figure who stood waiting tensely for him. Tarzan's bow and arrows lay out of reach where he had left them while showing off Sabor's hide. Now all he had to defend himself against the brutal strength of this great ape was his hunting knife.

As Kerchak came roaring toward him, Tarzan pulled his knife from its sheath and shouted his defiance. Tarzan knew that he did not dare to let Kerchak seize him in those heavy, powerful arms. Just as Kerchak was about to crash into him, Tarzan jumped aside. He caught one of the huge wrists as Kerchak passed, then drove his knife into Kerchak's body, just below the heart.

Before he could pull the blade free again, the ape lunged, wrenching the weapon out of his hands. Kerchak aimed a blow at the youth's head, one that would have crushed his skull if it had landed. But Tarzan was too nimble; ducking, he struck a double-handed blow into the pit of Kerchak's stomach.

The ape staggered, and with the mortal wound that Tarzan's knife had given him, he almost collapsed. Then, with a last mighty effort, he threw his enormous arms around Tarzan and held him in a crushing embrace. Straining to pull the boy toward him, Kerchak tried to sink his teeth into Tarzan's throat, but the young lord's strong fingers were at Kerchak's own throat before the teeth could reach him.

They struggled in a death grip, Kerchak trying to crush his opponent's life with his terrible strength, and Tarzan trying to choke the ape while he held the snarling mouth away. Slowly the ape's greater strength began to close the gap between them, and Kerchak's teeth came within barely an inch of Tarzan's throat. But then, with a shuddering tremor, the ape's heavy body stiffened and sank limply to the ground.

Kerchak was dead.

Tarzan pulled his knife out of Kerchak's chest. And then, as he had done with Sabor, he put a foot on the body of his vanquished enemy and his wild cry of victory rang through the forest. One by one the apes came to him and turned their backs in a gesture of submission.

And that was how young Lord Greystoke became king of the apes.

For months afterward the life of the ape band went on much as it had before. Tarzan's intelligence and his ability as a hunter kept them better fed than ever, and most of them were content with their new leader. He even began to lead them into the fields of the villagers. There they would forage at night while he climbed over the wall to collect the supply of arrows and eat the food that he had quickly discovered were always waiting there.

After some months the villagers began to grow discouraged that unseen creatures were stealing the bounty of their fields, and unnerved that the spirit they made their offering to actually came into their village to take it. Like many peoples who had lived close to the land for generations, the villagers held nature in great respect and awe. It was easy for them to believe that trees, animals, rivers, and the unpredictable earth itself had spirits and magical powers. But as long as the proper rituals were observed, such spirits would never violate a people's very home, as they were doing now. This was unheard of, and the villagers' new life here was beginning to seem as bad in its way as their old one.

At last even Mbonga, the headman, decided that they should look for another place to settle. So hunters began to roam deeper and deeper into the ape band's territory, looking for a better site. More and more often the apes were disturbed by their intrusions. Eventually the entire village moved to a place right in the heart of the band's home.

The creatures of the jungle had evolved a wary pattern of coexistence among their own. But when human beings moved into their territory, the natural order of their lives was violently disrupted, and if they could, they retreated from the threat. The jungle animals fled humans the way humans fled a plague, to reestablish their old, familiar habits in new, unsettled territory.

For a while Tarzan's ape band lingered because Tarzan could not bring himself to leave the cabin on the beach with all its treasures. But one day several of the apes found the new village growing right on the bank of a river that had been one of their watering places for generations; and so Tarzan led them inland for many days, to a spot untouched by any human being.

Once every moon Tarzan would travel back alone to spend a day with his books. He would also spy on the villagers and then replenish his supply of arrows. The fact that he did this only once a month, and that their fields lay unraided, was enough to convince the villagers that their new home was safe enough.

Because they did stay, Tarzan worried that someday they would find his cabin on the beach and take his beloved books away. He began to spend more and more time watching over his parents' cabin, and less and less time with the band, until some of the apes began to complain about his neglect.

So he spent the next month with them, hunting, eating, sleeping, and settling their endless squabbles over food. But by the end of the month Tarzan's restlessness had become almost unbearable. He longed for the cabin by the sea and the books that he never tired of reading and rereading. Since Kala's death and the arrival of the villagers, he had begun to realize how much he had grown away from the apes. Their minds had not kept pace with his, and he knew by now that they could never understand the strange and wonderful thoughts that filled his own mind more and more. He could not make them share his excitement at the idea of a world beyond their jungle, full of creatures like himself who lived in houses that moved from place to place, who had tools far better than sticks, and words for everything. He could not make them see why he wanted to find these creatures. He could not talk to the apes about his ideas or even his growing frustration and loneliness.

If Kala had still been alive, Tarzan would have been content to stay with the band forever, for her sake. But now that she was dead and his childhood playmates had grown into dull, surly adults, he began to think that simply living alone with his books, in the peace and solitude of his cabin, would be a much happier life than enduring this increasingly irritating and monotonous life as leader of the apes. And yet he stayed, out of a sense of responsibility and out of the habits of a lifetime . . . and because he knew that to live completely alone would not answer his questions about how other human beings lived, or change the feelings that burned inside him either.

And then one day, as he traveled through the trees, returning from one of his now rare journeys to the cabin by the shore, he looked down past the roaring white curtain of a waterfall to see something he had never seen before—except in his books. It was a *ship,* the house-on-water that was a home for his own people.

He dropped recklessly through the branches, his heart leaping, until he found a tree where he could watch the ship. Looking down, he saw on the shore a gathering of men—black men, like the ones he knew, but also men with skin as light as his own. And women . . . and one woman among them with pale, shining hair, so like the picture in the locket he wore that he gave a small cry of astonishment.

He moved even closer through the trees, until he was almost directly above the group, which stood murmuring in their strange language and gesturing at the falls. Piles of equipment lay heaped around them, and they had already set up odd-looking huts with sides that billowed in the wind. Tarzan's excitement grew as he saw the party of Europeans up close. Not only was their skin pale, but they wore clothes that entirely covered their bodies, like the people in his books, and their floating house lay waiting in the water. Surely these must be his own people after so long!

As he watched them set up camp, Tarzan was especially fascinated by the young woman with hair the color of sunlight. Seeing her stirred yearnings in him that he had never known before, even when he looked at the portraits in his locket. After a time she wandered over toward the tree where he lay hidden, and he had to hold his breath to keep himself from calling out to her. He should have been afraid; but he longed for her to look up and see him so that he could meet her eyes, which would look so much like his own. . . .

"Jane!" One of the men, with silver hair and deep folds in his face, called out to her. She hesitated, turning back to the campsite to rejoin the others.

Tarzan gave a grunt of frustration. Looking after her, he suddenly realized that the shadows had grown long and blue, that night would soon be falling. He knew that he should return to his band—although somehow the thought was less urgent now, and less appealing, than it had ever seemed before.

Reluctantly he swung back up into the branches and went on his way, hurrying through the trees until he found the ape band preparing for the night. The apes greeted him as they always had, and went on with their nest building, as they always had. He could not tell them what he had seen that day, even though his mind and heart were bursting with it—and he knew that they would not care anyway.

For the first time in his life he thought about the future—about his life going on forever this way, with nothing changing and no questions answered. He thought of the people he had seen that day disappearing, like the ones whose pictures were in the locket he wore. That night he dreamed, and when he awoke he remembered his dream for the first time. He had dreamed about the girl with golden hair.

In the morning he called the apes together and said to them, "Tarzan is not an ape. He is not like his people. His ways are not their ways, and so Tarzan is going back to his own kind. You must choose another to lead you, for Tarzan will not come back." And then he leaped up into the trees with a final cry of farewell and began his journey back to the place by the waterfall.

He did not know how he would greet these strangers, or whether they would welcome him or kill him. But he was not afraid. His need was too strong. He was sure that he would find a way to communicate with them somehow.

Tarzan, young Lord Greystoke, king of the apes, was leaving his strange, wild life behind. He was about to begin a new life—one that would be far stranger and more wonderful than anything he had ever imagined.